D0119047

LITTLE TOOT
and the Lighthouse

Story concept *by* Linda Gramatky-Smith
***Illustrated by* Mark Weber**

Based on the character created by
HARDIE GRAMATKY

**Weekly Reader is a registered trademark of
Weekly Reader Corporation**

2002 Edition

A Grosset & Dunlap **ALL ABOARD BOOK**®

Library of Congress Cataloging-in-Publication Data
Gramatky-Smith, Linda.
Little Toot and the lighthouse / story concept created by Linda Gramatky-Smith ; Illustrated by Mark Weber.
p.   cm. — (All aboard books)   "Based on the character created by Hardie Gramatky."
Summary: Little Toot and his father take a trip to Maine, where Little Toot gets lost exploring with his friend Bob.
[1. Tugboats Fiction. 2. Lost children Fiction.] I. Weber, Mark (Mark A.), 1958- ill. II. Title. III. Series.
IV. Series: Grosset & Dunlap all aboard book.   PZ7.G76545Lit   1999   [E]—dc21   99-23220   CIP

Little Toot lived at the foot of an old, old wharf right in the middle of New York harbor. It was a busy place. Each day, Little Toot and the other tugboats would push big ships into the docks to be unloaded, or tow them out to the wide open seas.

It was hard work. But Little Toot loved every
minute of it. He loved riding the big ocean waves.
He loved to whistle *toot-toot-toot* to the ocean liners
and boats he recognized.

But sometimes Little Toot would look out to sea
and imagine all sorts of adventures beyond the
harbor waves.

"I want to see new things," he told his father, Big Toot. "I want to explore new places."

"That's a great idea," said Big Toot. "Why don't we take a trip? We can visit some friends in Maine."

"Yes!" cried Little Toot. He was so excited, balls of smoke puffed out of his candy-stick smokestack. The flag at his masthead danced in the breeze.

The next morning, Little Toot and Big Toot set out for the coast of Maine. They passed the beaches of Connecticut and Rhode Island. Big Toot pointed out bridges and fishing piers.

Once, Little Toot saw a long, noisy train snaking its way along the railroad tracks at the water's edge.

"Remember these tracks and bridges and piers. They all are landmarks," Big Toot explained. "We'll see them again on our trip back, and they'll help us find our way home."

When the sun started to go down, Big Toot and Little Toot anchored at Buzzards Bay for the night.

Early the next morning they set off again. It was a beautiful day. The water was calm, and friendly seagulls flew overhead. After a while they came up to a tall white lighthouse, its red light blinking brightly—six seconds on, six seconds off. It jutted out into the ocean, surrounded by big gray rocks. Little Toot stared up at it in awe.

"That's Nubble Light," said Big Toot. "That means we've arrived in Maine. It's not too much farther now!"

"Hooray!" cheered Little Toot.

A little farther on, Little Toot saw a beach dotted with pine trees. Families picnicked on the white sand, and children in brightly colored swimsuits tumbled in the ocean waves.

"Let's stop and play!" Little Toot said. But Big Toot didn't think that was a good idea. "We've come a long way," he said. "Let's explore later."

They traveled for a while longer and finally reached the dock where they would be staying. Fishing boats called hello to their dear friend Big Toot. Little Toot smiled at them all.

"Hi!" said a small rowboat, floating up to the tugboats. "My name is Bob."

Bob told Little Toot all about the fishing harbor.
He showed the tugboat the lobster traps stacked up
on the dock and the tidal pools where sea urchins
collected at low tide. Little Toot taught Bob how to
play thread-the-needle and how to cut figure 8's.

"What do you want to do now?" asked Bob.

"What about the pretty beach with the pine trees?" Little Toot asked eagerly. "Can you take me there?"

Bob spun around excitedly. "Which one do you mean?" he asked.

"I passed it on the way here," Little Toot explained. "Maybe we can explore it together."

Big Toot was busy laughing with some lobster boats, so Little Toot left without saying good-bye. He and Bob floated merrily out to the open sea. They splashed in the waves, spraying each other with water. Fishermen heading to check their lobster traps waved to the little boats. *Toot-toot-toot*, Little Toot whistled back.

Soon they spied the sparkling white beach.
The two boats bobbed along close to the shore.
Little Toot sent out a volley of smoke balls as
a greeting.

The children laughed and waved and shouted happily to the boats. Little Toot and Bob darted around in wide figure 8's. They couldn't help but show off a bit. It was so much fun. The friends played by the beach for hours.

Then Little Toot noticed that shadows were starting to lengthen as the sun began to set. The sky was lit with a beautiful red glow. Families started packing up blankets and towels, getting ready to leave.

"We'd better hurry and go back to the dock," Little Toot told Bob. "No one knows where we are."

"Okay!" said Bob. Then he frowned. "But which way do we go?"

Little Toot looked around. He and Bob floated near some big rocks. To the left of the rocks, he saw a red buoy. To the right, he glimpsed a yellow buoy. Neither looked familiar. He'd been too busy peering at the beach to notice anything nearby.

"I-I'm not sure which way to go," Little Toot stammered. A chilly wind blew, and the boats shivered. The sun dipped below the horizon, and the day grew darker still.

"I want to go home!" Bob said. He began to cry.

Little Toot wanted to find his father. He didn't want to be out on the cold, dark ocean, lost and afraid and very far from home. A tear rolled down his cheek. But then he took a deep breath. *I'm wasting time*, he told himself. *I've got to be brave for Bob. I've got to think things through.*

"Let's go this way!" Little Toot declared, motioning toward the red buoy. The two friends floated past the buoy, and the waves grew rougher.

Is this right? Little Toot wondered. *Is this the way to go?*

"Look!" Bob said with a squeal. "There's a lighthouse ahead!"

A lighthouse! Little Toot peered into the darkness and saw the blinking red light. Why, it was Nubble Light—the same lighthouse he and Big Toot had passed on their way to the dock! Little Toot stopped so suddenly, Bob bumped into him.

"That lighthouse is a landmark!" Little Toot said. "It will help us find our way back."

Little Toot took a deep breath. He thought hard about landmarks—everything he and Bob had passed on their way to the beach.

They hadn't passed the lighthouse, that was for sure. So this must be the wrong direction!

"The dock is the other way!" Little Toot told his friend. "Let's turn around, and we'll be back before we know it!"

The boats drifted past the beach and the yellow buoy. And soon they passed a big silver buoy, its bell ringing. "Yes!" Little Toot said. "I remember seeing *this* landmark on the way to the beach."

And there, up ahead, was the dock.
He could see Big Toot waving his flag.

"Thank goodness you're okay!" Big Toot said when the boats neared the dock. "You know, you should always tell me before you take off like that. We all were so worried!"

Before Little Toot could explain, Bob piped up. "We went to the beach with the pine trees. We played games and made the children laugh and had so much fun! But then we got lost. I was scared. But Little Toot was so brave. He saved us!"

"Weren't you afraid too?" a fishing boat asked
Little Toot.

"Nope!" Little Toot said proudly. Then he paused
a moment. If Big Toot hadn't taught him about
landmarks, he wouldn't have found his way back.

"Well, maybe a little," he admitted with a grin.

When their vacation was over, Little Toot and Big Toot set off for home. Little Toot led the way past beaches, train tracks, fishing piers, and bridges. *Toot-toot-toot*, he whistled at each landmark. "I know exactly how to go!"